PENALTY SHOT

THE SLATER LIBRARY
And Fanning Annex
26 Main Street
Jewett City, CT 06351

The #1
Sports Series
for Kids

MATT CHRISTOPHER®

PENALTY SHOT

LITTLE, BROWN AND COMPANY

New York ❧ Boston

Copyright © 1997 by Matt Christopher Royalties, Inc.

All rights reserved. Except as permitted under the U.S. Copyright Act of 1976 no part of this publication may be reproduced, distributed, or transmitted in any form or by any means, or stored in a database or retrieval system, without the prior written permission of the publisher.

Little, Brown and Company

Hachette Book Group USA
1271 Avenue of Americas, New York, NY 10020
Visit our Web site at www.lb-kids.com

www.mattchristopher.com

First Paperback Edition

The characters and events portrayed in this book are fictitious. Any similarity to real persons, living or dead, is coincidental and not intended by the author.

Matt Christopher® is a registered trademark of Matt Christopher Royalties, Inc.

Library of Congress Cataloging-in-Publication Data

Christopher, Matt.
  Penalty shot / by Matt Christopher — 1st ed.
    p.   cm.
  Summary: Jeff, already worried about losing his place on the hockey team because of low grades, suddenly finds himself the victim of sabotage in the form of forged papers.
    ISBN 0-316-14190-9
    [1. Hockey — Fiction.   2. Mystery and detective stories.]
  I. Title.
PZ7.M43159Pe   1997
[Fic] — dc20   96-9741

20 19 18 17 16 15 14 13 12 11 10

COM-MO

Printed in the United States of America

To Brad, Mame, Tyler, and Jeremy

PENALTY SHOT

1

Oof!

He recovers from a block by a burly defenseman.

He's in the clear.

The puck is coming his way.

He positions his hockey stick and traps it.

Slap. Tap. Tap.

He lines it up.

For a split second, there's a clearing between him and the goal.

The goalie reaches high.

He shoots low.

Smack!

1

The puck careens across the ice.

It shoots by the goalie and hits the back of the cage.

Goal!

Jeff Connors raised his arms in victory. His breath came out in a fog in the crisp winter air. It was his second imaginary goal so far and he wasn't even halfway to the rink. If he could do as well when he actually got on the ice, he'd be a shoo-in to make the hockey team.

He'd made the team the year before, no problem. It hadn't been his playing ability that had kept him out of uniform. No, everyone, even the coach, had been sorry he'd been sidelined.

Jeff was willing to take some of the blame for what had happened. But he hadn't had much sympathy from the one person who could have kept him on the ice. And how was he supposed to feel about that?

Just thinking about Mr. Pearson made him angry all over again. Even now he could hear the tired tone in his English teacher's voice. "Well, Mr. Connors," he had said, "it seems you chose not to heed my last warning. I told you the consequences would be grave if you didn't. Much as I hated to do it, I fear you left me with no choice but to send a full report of your current grades to your coach."

Jeff still felt as though he'd swallowed a lump of hot coal when he remembered the conversation he'd had with his coach later that day.

"Mr. Pearson tells me you knew your grades were slipping," Coach Wallace had said, shaking his head, "but that you didn't do anything about it. At least, not that he could see. Well, rules are rules. And the

number one rule of this school's sports program is that if your grades fall behind, then
you're off the team. I'm sorry, Jeff, but you'll
have to turn in your uniform."

So that afternoon, while all his teammates
were lacing up their skates and joking around
in the locker room, Jeff had quietly emptied
his locker. He had pretended not to notice
how the room fell silent as one by one his
friends realized what he was doing. The
one-mile walk home that day had felt like
twenty.

Jeff shook his head. That was then and
this is now, he thought. Mom, Dad, and the
coach are willing to give me another chance.
And I'm doing okay this year.

He tried not to think about the English
composition he'd put off writing yesterday.
Or the spelling and reading comprehension
test he'd taken two days before. If he didn't
do well on them . . .

2

Jeff put all thoughts of tests and compositions out of his head. Instead, he continued his make-believe game. As he bobbed and weaved down the street, stick in ready position and his gear bag balanced over his shoulder, he was in a world of his own.

The puck curled around the boards behind the net and slid free of the tangle of players nearby. It was getting closer. He just had to dodge this one defenseman and it was his. With a quick lateral move and a jab of his stick —

"Grrrrrrr . . ."

The sound of a deep, low growl brought Jeff back to reality. He wasn't on the ice facing a defenseman. He was on the sidewalk of a tree-lined street, facing the biggest, meanest-looking dog he'd ever seen!

Jeff sprang back. The dog eyed him, baring its fangs, but didn't move.

As a five-year-old, Jeff had been bitten by a dog. He'd been nervous around dogs ever since. He usually avoided them so that people wouldn't notice. That way, he didn't have to explain anything to anyone.

Jeff hiked up his duffel bag and was about to move away when he heard a familiar voice call his name.

"Hey, Jeff, you're not going to leave without me, are you?"

It was his friend Kevin Leach. Jeff realized he was standing right in front of the Leaches' house.

Kevin hurried out the front door, stick in

hand. At the same time, the dog spun around and charged. Jeff watched in horror as it jumped up at Kevin's face. He was powerless to do anything to help his friend!

To his amazement, Kevin broke out laughing and shoved the dog aside.

"So I see you've met Ranger," he said, grinning from ear to ear. "Ranger, this is Jeff. Jeff's my oldest buddy, so I want you two to get on real well, okay, boy?"

As if he understood, Ranger turned his massive head toward Jeff. Jeff took a step back.

"When did you get a dog?" he asked.

"My dad surprised me last night," said Kevin. "Some guy at his office moved and couldn't take Ranger with him, so Dad brought him home. As soon as Ranger saw me, he came right over and started licking my hand. That did it."

"I'll bet," Jeff said uneasily. He couldn't

imagine anyone liking a dog licking their hand. To have those teeth so close . . .

"Luckily, Mom likes him, too. I'll feed him and walk him before school, but she's going to take him for walks during the day and when I'm at hockey practice. If I make the team, that is."

"You'll make it," Jeff said, happy to change the subject. Although they were the same age, Kevin wasn't built as sturdily as Jeff. In fact, there were times he looked downright skinny. But he was a good defenseman and he loved hockey almost as much as Jeff. "You just have to do as well as you did last year and you'll be on the team again. Hope-fully, I'll be there with you."

"You'd be a shoo-in for right wing if you hadn't been thrown off —" Kevin stopped abruptly. He shot Jeff an apologetic look. "Sorry," he mumbled.

Jeff's ears burned. "Yeah, well, that was

last year. I'm not going to get thrown off the team this year. So you'd better be ready to back me up on the ice again!" He punched Kevin in the shoulder.

"*Grrrrr . . .*"

Jeff jumped back. Kevin laid a hand on Ranger's head and told the dog to shush. Then he looked curiously at Jeff. "He's a really relaxed dog, but he's been taught to protect his owner. Sometimes he gets spooked by sudden movements. He doesn't bite or anything. So you don't have to be scared of him, Jeff."

"Oh, I wasn't," Jeff said.

Kevin cocked an eyebrow at him. "Jeff, I know you don't like dogs, remember? But Ranger is different. You'll see that, once you get to know him."

Just then, Mrs. Leach opened the door. "You boys are going to be late if you don't get going," she called. "Ranger, come here!"

9

As Ranger bounded inside, Jeff and Kevin gathered up their gear and headed off to the rink. Kevin talked on and on about how great it was to have a dog. Though Jeff barely listened to the words, he heard one thing loud and clear: if Kevin had his way, he and Ranger would be inseparable. And if Jeff couldn't get over his fear, what would that do to their friendship?

3

Jeff pushed that thought out of his mind. He needed to get focused on what was ahead — the last day of hockey tryouts.

"I'll give you five-to-one odds," he said to Kevin as they hurried toward the skating rink.

"On what?"

"On you making the team."

Kevin grinned. "Okay, but if I'm five to one, you must be two to one. Coach Wallace has had you in the starting string practically all week. You're on the squad, no question."

"Don't I wish. You know who's a sure bet, don't you?"

The boys looked at each other and in the same breath said, "Bucky Ledbetter!"

"Talk about skating," Kevin added.

"Yeah, he's good, all right," agreed Jeff. "I just wish he wouldn't let everyone know it all the time."

Kevin shook his head. "He's loud and cocky, that's for sure. I wouldn't want to get on his bad side. He'd be one tough enemy."

"Aw, he's not so tough," said Jeff. "I tell you, though, if he ever said to me the things he says to his brother, I don't know what I'd do."

"Hayes? Boy, there's a guy who's having a tough time on the ice!"

Jeff nodded. "Bucky's mouthing at him probably doesn't help. It's funny, I heard the coach say Hayes'd be a decent player if he'd just concentrate more. I bet that's why he didn't make the team last year."

They mounted the steps to the rink. As they headed for the locker room, Kevin said, "Guess all that really matters is that we get the chance to show the coach what a dynamic duo we are together. You at right wing with me right behind you. Right?"

"Right!"

The locker room was already crowded with boys lacing up their skates and pulling on their pads. Jeff and Kevin hurried to join them. In no time at all, they were on the ice.

Coach Wallace blew his whistle.

"Okay, guys, this is it," the coach announced.

"The last day of tryouts. I'm not going to bore you with the usual speech about how I wish I could put all of you on the team, even though that's the truth." A few of the boys muttered and others hung their heads. "What you should know, however, is that I've decided to try something new this year." The same boys perked up again. "I'm going to keep two promising players on as alternates. They'll practice with the team and come to the games, though they'll only play if nobody else on the team can. This may sound like a lousy position to take. But consider how much stronger you'll be next year, going into tryouts with a whole season of practices under your belt. And here's something else to think about: if for any reason I feel there's someone on the team who's slacking off, I won't hesitate to substitute one of the alternates in his place. Now get out there and warm up!"

As Jeff took to the ice, he knew his face was beet red. A few guys glanced his way, then quickly dropped their eyes. Jeff was sure everyone there was thinking the same thing: this year, if he got kicked off the team, he wouldn't be missed. Someone else would be more than happy to step in. And more than ready.

4

After ten minutes of warm-up, Coach Wallace whistled the players back in line. He had them count off as either "in" or "out," then told the two groups to form circles at center ice.

"Here's the drill," he said. "I'm going to start the puck toward one of you. I want you to stop it, then pass it on to someone else. Don't skate after it. Just keep it moving. If you have to skate, if you miss the puck, or if you slip and fall, drop out and head for the sideline."

Coach Wallace gave a puck to the "out"

group, then joined the "ins." He dropped the puck in front of himself and shot it to Shep Fredrickson. Shep stopped it carefully. He glanced around the ring and eased a pass to Michael Gillis. It slid right up to Michael's stick.

This looks like a breeze, Jeff thought as he watched Michael pass to Bucky Ledbetter.

Still, he remained alert, his stick in ready position.

It was a good thing he did. Bucky flipped a fast but accurate pass to Chad Galbraith, but Chad was caught napping. Coach Wallace motioned to him to skate aside. Bucky retrieved the puck and fired a lightning-quick shot right at Jeff.

Jeff reacted instantly. He stopped the puck with just enough give to keep it from bouncing back into the middle of the ring. He sent a controlled pass across to Hayes.

After that, the competitive juices began to

flow as each player tried to outsmart his opponents. One player after another had to leave the circle. Soon there were only four players left: Bucky Ledbetter, Shep Fredrickson, Michael Gillis, and Jeff.

Bucky had just received a pass from Shep when Coach Wallace blew his whistle. Jeff glanced over at the coach, ready to learn about the next drill.

Wham!

Out of nowhere came a pass so hard and powerful it almost knocked the stick from his hands. As the puck skittered away, Jeff looked back to the circle in disbelief. Bucky was grinning at him.

"Sure you're ready for this, Connors?" Bucky asked snidely. "A season away from the squad seems to have dulled your reactions."

Jeff had opened his mouth to reply when

the coach called for him to retrieve the puck. With a last backward glance, Jeff skated down the ice, scooped up the disk, and hurried back to hear what the coach was telling the other players.

"Okay, same two groups," he said. "Outs, you split in half again, eight to a goal. Choose six guys to rotate in as defensemen, one player at a time. The remaining two guys will take turns playing goalie. Got it?"

The outs nodded and skated off.

"Ins, form three lines at mid-ice at the right-wing, center, and left-wing spots. Half face one goal, half the other. Your job is to get by the defenseman and take a shot on goal if you can. Easy does it on the goalie, okay? I don't want any injuries. After your run down the ice, skate back and get ready to attack the opposite goal. Got it?"

The ins nodded and scrambled to form

their lines. In less than a minute, the drill started.

Jeff's heart raced with excitement. Sometimes practice could be dull, but drills like this really gave players a chance to shine.

His group was up first. Jeff was in the right-wing slot. When he saw that Bucky was in center, his enthusiasm flagged a bit. Then he shook his head, reminding himself that he and Bucky might be on the line together on the team. He had to start working well with him, just in case.

Coach Wallace blew his whistle, signaling them to begin the drill. Bucky's brother, Hayes, was at left wing. He took a pass from Bucky, then tried to shoot the puck across the ice to Jeff.

It didn't make it. Kevin skated in and stole it.

Bucky groaned. "Good move, little brother, real good move! Why don't you just pass it to the other team next time and save us all the trouble of trying to set up a play?"

He skated to the sidelines in disgust. Jeff followed him.

"Hey, Bucky, lighten up! We all send bad passes, you know," he said.

"Hayes can take the criticism. He knows I want him to get a fair crack at a place on the team this year. Unlike *last* year, when he was beaten out by someone who couldn't stick it out." Bucky cast a sidelong glance at Jeff that spoke volumes.

Jeff reddened. Darn that Bucky! He makes it sound as if I got kicked off the team on purpose!

But he swallowed his anger and skated back in line. For the rest of the afternoon he concentrated on playing as hard as he could. As a result, he made few mistakes and left practice feeling that he had given it his best shot. Now it was up to the coach to decide if

Jeff was worth giving a second chance. Jeff knew he'd have his answer in less than twenty-four hours. Coach Wallace would post the team roster for all to see sometime the next day.

5

Hi, Mom!" Jeff called out from the mud-room next to the kitchen. "Anybody home?"

"Mom's at the dentist," came a voice from upstairs. "There're some killer brownies she just made on the counter. Oh, yeah, and there's a letter for you. She put it on your bed."

"Thanks, Candy," he called back to his sister. Candy was a few years older than he was. Her life revolved around her friends in high school. Still, they had a warm relationship most of the time.

As he hung up his coat and walked into the kitchen, he wondered about the letter. He had just taken a bite out of one of the brownies when he realized who it must be from. He raced up the stairs two at a time.

There on his pillow lay a big envelope. The return address read "The National Hockey League," along with a team name and address in red-and-blue letters. With a yelp, Jeff tore it open. A glossy black-and-white photo fell out. It was a picture of his favorite player, Eric Stone! Jeff had written to the team's fan club more than a month ago. He had started to think his letter had been lost. But here was the photo, signed and everything!

Jeff propped the picture up on his desk and was about to crumple up the envelope when a piece of paper fell out. He picked it up and stared at it, not believing what he saw. It was a letter, written to him by Eric Stone himself!

Jeff sat on the bed and read it.

Dear Jeff,

Thank you for your letter telling me how much you enjoy watching me play my favorite game — hockey. It makes it all the more exciting for me knowing that there are fans like you out there rooting for me and my team. I hope I'll live up to your expectations this season and not do anything to let you down.

Being a good hockey player takes a lot of practice. Since you say that you might want to be a professional hockey player, too, let me give you a little hint. It's not just how well you skate and handle a stick. No, you have to be a smart player, too, to get ahead in this

game. That means you need a good educa-
tion. That's the best way to train your mind
to learn everything you have to know as a
pro.

 So work hard out there on the ice, but
work just as hard in the classroom. Remem-
ber: keep your grades up and your stick
down!

All the best,
Eric Stone

As Jeff read through the letter, he felt his excitement drain away. "Keep your grades up!" "Train your mind!" It was as if Eric Stone knew Jeff had had trouble in school before.

Then he began to wonder: had there been some mistakes in the letter he'd written to Eric? Maybe a misspelled word or a grammar problem? It hadn't been a very long letter but, still, he knew it was likely it had been riddled with "sentence faults" and "paragraph faults," as his teacher called them.

Why didn't I ask Candy to look over the letter before I sent it? He groaned inwardly. But he knew why. He would have felt like a little kid just learning to write. He hated feeling stupid.

Jeff took one last look at Eric Stone's letter, then crumpled it slowly in his hand. A quick toss and it was headed for the wastebasket — just as Candy walked into the room. The letter bounced off her knee and to the floor.

"Whoa, I'm unarmed!" Candy joked. She scooped up the wad and was about to toss it back at him. Then she stopped and smoothed out the paper. "Isn't this the NHL emblem? Are they writing to you to say you've been selected as the number one draft pick?"

"Very funny," said Jeff, trying to act as though it were nothing. "Here, give it to me."

But Candy was already reading the letter. Jeff turned his back on her and picked up one of his schoolbooks.

After a moment, Candy said, "I don't get it. Eric Stone is your big hero, isn't he? So how come you're throwing away a letter from him? That's better than an autograph on a program, even."

Jeff spun around and replied, "Yeah, you're right. I wasn't thinking. Maybe I will keep it after all."

Candy held it out to him but before she let go, she asked quietly, "Are you upset about what he said about the importance of doing well in school?"

Jeff snatched the paper out of her hand and stalked over to the desk, not answering her question.

"Because if you are, I'm sure you could do better with a little extra help. Mom and Dad said they'd get you a student tutor if —"

"I don't need a tutor! I'm not stupid!" Jeff said angrily. "I just need a little peace and quiet so I can get to work on my composition. It's due tomorrow and I don't want to spend all night on it." He tore a fresh sheet of paper out of his three-ring binder and sat at his desk.

"I didn't say you were stupid," Candy said as she left the room. "At least, I don't think you're stupid in the way *you* think I mean." She slammed the door behind her.

Jeff stared at the photo of Eric Stone for a few minutes. Then, with a sigh, he turned the picture over, picked up his pencil, and tired to remember everything the teacher had told the class about writing a composition.

The clock on his wall ticked loudly. Downstairs, he heard his mother come in the back door. A truck drove by the window. Eventually, he heard his father's car turn into the driveway. Soon it would be time for dinner.

The paper was still blank when he pushed himself back from the desk and headed downstairs.

Oh, well, he thought. I'll give it another try later. After I eat.

6

Is the roster up yet?" Kevin asked breathlessly as he hurried into school Friday morning. Jeff yawned widely before answering. He had stayed up late the night before finishing his composition.

"Not yet," he replied. The rink was next to the school and he had just had time to stop by on his way to school. But the list hadn't been tacked to the door. Now they would have to get permission at lunch recess to check again.

Morning classes dragged by. At lunch, Jeff sat with Kevin and a few other hockey players, but he was too nervous to eat more than a sandwich and a banana. He wasn't the only one. When the bell signaled the half hour of after-lunch free time, everyone at the table jumped up as if he'd been stuck with pins.

"I'll get the okay from Ms. Collins," Jeff said as he headed over to the teacher on duty.

Ms. Collins agreed that they could take a quick walk to the rink to see if the roster was up. As he moved to rejoin the others, Jeff heard her call out to him.

"I'll see you in English class, Jeff. I'm looking forward to reading your composition."

In the excitement, Jeff had almost forgotten about it. Well, he'd stayed up half the night working on it, so no one could accuse him of not trying. Still, as he gave Ms. Collins a half wave to show he'd heard her, he felt a knot tighten in his stomach.

No time for that now, he thought. He sprinted to catch up with the rest of the boys. Together they hurried to the rink.

The list was there! Jeff pushed his way forward and scanned it for his name. At first he didn't see it. Then he read through the roster again — and there it was! He let out a sigh of relief.

Kevin, Bucky, and Hayes had all made the squad, too. So had most of the other players from the year before. There were a few new names, too, including two way down at the bottom under the heading of "Alternates." At the very bottom of the page was a note telling players there would be no practice that day but that they should stop in and get their uniforms.

Jeff ran down the steps and searched for Kevin. He spotted him with Bucky, Hayes, and a fourth fellow he didn't recognize.

"Hey there, fellow Blades!" he called.

Kevin was all smiles as Jeff clapped him on the back.

"Hey yourself," he replied. "We were just talking about getting in a little weekend practice down at the pond. Interested?"

"Sure, sounds good," said Jeff. He glanced curiously at the new person.

Kevin introduced the two to each other. "Jeff Connors, this is Sam Metcalf. He just moved here. He's going to be the team manager!"

Jeff shook Sam's hand. "That name sounds familiar," he said.

Sam shrugged. "If you read the local district sports pages, you might have seen it in a few columns about hockey last year. I led my old team in scoring. I had hoped I'd be able to play here, too. But I missed the tryouts for the Blades because we were moving."

Jeff shook his head sympathetically.

"That's rough," he said. He was going to ask Sam some more questions but was cut off by the bell.

As the boys headed back to school, they settled on a time to meet for a pick-up game on the pond on Saturday.

"I'll be there," Jeff promised. "But now I have to turn in my English composition." He groaned.

"Something the matter?" Sam asked.

"Jeff has trouble writing," Hayes cut in before Jeff had a chance to speak.

Sam shot Jeff a sideways glance but didn't say anything.

Jeff reddened. "Yeah, well, Hayes is so good at it he thinks anyone who doesn't get all A's has a problem. He's lucky."

Hayes smiled at him and nodded. "You're right. I am lucky."

❉   ❉   ❉

35

Jeff was the last one to arrive in class. He turned in his composition and began to struggle to keep his mind from wandering. He liked Ms. Collins and really did want to do well in her class. But the afternoon sun was slanting through the tall classroom windows. Jeff found himself staring at the dust whirling in the sunbeam and daydreaming.

I sure hope it doesn't snow, he thought. It'll be easier to play on the pond tomorrow if we don't have to clear the ice. I wonder if I'll be able to get the same number on my uniform that I had last year?

At last, the bell rang. As Jeff hurried out of the room, he could feel Ms. Collins's eyes on his back. But she didn't call for him to stay.

The final two classes breezed by quickly. Jeff grabbed the books he needed for his weekend homework, threw on his coat, and ran over to the rink. With all the other newly appointed Blades, he stood in line to receive his uniform.

"Welcome back to the team," Coach Wallace said as he handed him a bright yellow jersey with a 19 on the back. Sam Metcalf noted the number in the book he was holding, then handed the book to Jeff for his signature. As Jeff was signing, Coach Wallace added, "I hope I'll see that number on the ice the whole season this year, not folded away like last year."

"Yes, sir!" Jeff answered with an enthusiastic nod. "You can count on it!"

I hope, he added silently. He gathered up his uniform and moved aside for the next in line. I sure do hope so.

7

Saturday dawned bright, crisp, and clear. Jeff jumped out of bed, dressed quickly, and pounded down the stairs to the mudroom. He was throwing equipment into his duffel when Candy wandered in.

"I wondered what that racket was!" she said with a yawn.

Jeff answered, "I'm meeting the guys for a game, but we have to get there early before someone else gets the best spot!"

"Well, eat something first," his mother called out as he barged into the kitchen.

Obediently, he wolfed down a bowl of cereal before heading out the door.

Ten minutes later he met up with the rest of the guys at the pond. It was still early in the day. With a little luck, they'd have a good couple of hours before the pond filled up with skaters. The only damper on his enjoyment was Ranger. Kevin had tied the big dog to a tree, but even so, Jeff was on the ice — and away from the dog — before anyone else.

They all took time to warm up, but before long Bucky called them together to choose teams. There were six boys in all, which meant they could go three-on-three. Bucky selected Hayes and Shep. Jeff, Kevin, and Chad made up the other side.

Since they didn't have an extra guy to drop the puck for a face-off, they threw fingers to see who would be on offense first. Bucky's side won. As they skated into position, Jeff, Kevin, and Chad called out for their men.

"I've got Shep!" Kevin said. Chad yelled that Hayes was his. That left Bucky for Jeff.

"Remember, no rough stuff!" Kevin reminded them as Bucky's team started down the ice. "We don't want any injuries before the season even starts!"

The trick with playing three-on-three without a goalie was to keep the offense from getting a clear shot. Anticipating a pass, stealing the puck off a stick, and crowding your player out of position were the keys to getting the puck headed the other way.

Bucky brought the puck down the ice with control. But Jeff stuck with him, looking for any opportunity to snag the disk away from him. Bucky was forced to make a pass; Hayes missed it completely. With a crow of victory, Chad snapped it up and skated furiously down the ice undefended. He drew up

40

short right in front of the goal and casually slid the puck between the stakes.

"Hayes! Why didn't you chase him?" Bucky yelled.

Hayes poked his stick at the ice. "I knew I couldn't catch him," he said lamely.

Bucky shook his head angrily. "You always have to *try*. If you give up too easily, the other team will *always* beat you."

Though Jeff agreed that Hayes should have tried harder, he didn't like the way Bucky was talking to his younger brother. He had started to tell Bucky to cool off when Chad skated up with the puck.

"Care to try again?" he said with a devilish grin and a wag of his eyebrows. Everyone broke up laughing, even Bucky.

"Be prepared," was all Bucky said as he took the disk.

Bucky started with the puck again. This time, he skated in long strides to the very

41

edge of the ice, then spun around and passed to the middle, where Shep was waiting. Kevin was caught off guard and couldn't cover his man. Shep controlled the puck easily and streaked toward the goal. Jeff made a split-second decision. He left Bucky wide open and went after Shep, yelling, "Switch!" to indicate that Kevin should get on Bucky.

But Bucky was too quick. The minute Jeff stopped covering him, he skated furiously toward the goal. Too late, Jeff realized what was about to happen. Shep glanced up, found his teammate, and slapped a pass to him seconds before Jeff reached him. It was pinpoint accurate. All Bucky had to do was deflect the puck into the goal to tie the score.

"That good enough for you?" Bucky challenged Chad with a smile.

Chad shrugged. "If I'd been involved in the play, I'm guessing I'd be taking the puck down the ice solo again. But I'm sure Jeff and Kevin did all they could." He sighed dramatically while his teammates rolled their eyes.

The two teams traded goals and good-humored jibes for another hour. Only when Bucky criticized Hayes for not playing aggressively enough did the friendly atmosphere dissolve. It was after one such comment that Jeff called for a break.

The hungry boys crowded onto the bench and shared the snacks they'd brought.

"So where do you think Coach will put each of us this year?" Chad asked around a mouthful of crackers.

"I'll probably be at center again," Bucky said.

"I'd like to be at wing," Hayes piped in.

"Ha! If you keep playing the way you've been playing today, the only place you'll be is on the bench!" Bucky snorted.

Jeff couldn't believe that Bucky had said something so mean to Hayes right in front of them. He half wished Hayes would tell Bucky off, but Hayes was silent. The other boys were suddenly busy with their laces or rummaging in their duffels for more snacks.

Kevin stood up and wiped the crumbs from his coat. "I'm going to let Ranger run around for a while, okay?" he said as he undid the leash.

Before Jeff had a chance to protest, Ranger wriggled free of Kevin's grasp and bounded over to the bench. He nosed each boy in turn, looking for a treat. They all patted him and pushed him away. When he reached Jeff, Jeff dropped the cookie he was holding as if it had burned his fingers.

Ranger snapped it up and gulped it down in one bite.

Licking his chops and panting, he took a hopeful step toward Jeff.

Jeff shrank back into the bench.

"Jeff, what's wrong? You're not afraid of the dog, are you?" Chad asked.

Kevin collared Ranger and tugged him away from Jeff.

"'Course I'm not afraid," Jeff said, embarrassed. "I just didn't like the smell of his breath, that's all."

Chad nodded his head seriously. "Must have been the cookie Shep's mom made. That was the last thing Ranger ate!"

All the guys laughed, but Jeff caught a look exchanged between Bucky and Hayes. The look seemed to say that neither boy believed it had been bad breath that had made Jeff jump.

8

By the time they had reassembled on the ice, several other skaters had joined them. Mothers with children just trying out skates for the first time, solo skaters doing fancy moves, and another group of hockey players vied for position on the small space.

"Hey, isn't that Sam Metcalf over there?" said Bucky, pointing to the second hockey group.

Kevin shaded his eyes and nodded. "You wanna see if they'd be up for getting a real game going? Looks like they have about six players, too."

"Good idea." Bucky skated off.

While they waited, Shep, Kevin, and Chad passed the puck back and forth. Jeff decided to let Hayes know he didn't approve of what Bucky had said earlier.

"Hey, Hayes," he began.

Hayes held up his hand. "Listen, I know what you're going to say. But don't worry about me. Before tryouts began, I asked my brother to keep me on my toes this year. Even though he's kind of a jerk about it, he's just trying to help me be a better player."

"But you're on the team already," Jeff persisted. "So why do you need him to keep razzing you like that?"

Hayes gave Jeff a lopsided grin. "You may have forgotten about those two alternates, but I haven't. I may be on the team now, but that's no guarantee I'll stay on it." Jeff was about to give Hayes a word of encouragement when the other hockey team skated up. As they started introducing themselves to the others, Hayes added one last comment.

"I would have thought you, out of anybody, would understand I don't want to be yanked from the roster. You know, since you have experience with that."

Jeff wanted the pond to open up and swallow him. Instead, a gloved hand grasped his and shook it.

Sam Metcalf was grinning at him. "Did you hear the news?" he said excitedly. "I'm officially an alternate for the team now! One of the guys who was chosen decided he would play for an intramural squad instead, so Coach Wallace promoted me from manager to player."

Jeff smiled warmly. "That's great!" he said, liking Sam's enthusiasm. In fact, he decided he liked Sam, period. It was a feeling that grew through the afternoon as the two teams battled for the puck. Sam was a good player, confident in his own abilities but generous with his praise for his teammates. By the time the sun was setting, Jeff found himself wishing Sam had been promoted to full player instead of just alternate.

But in order for that to happen, one of the existing players would have to go. Much as he liked Sam, Jeff didn't want that to happen.

9

Two days later, Jeff found himself wishing he were back on the ice. The minute he walked into English class Monday afternoon, he knew something was wrong.

"Jeff, could I see you for a minute?" Ms. Collins asked quietly. She handed him the composition he'd written the week before. It was covered with green correction marks — and a big, fat "E."

Jeff waited for his teacher to lecture him. But she didn't. Instead, she handed him a slip of paper. "This is the name of a tutor. You have a choice: work with her to improve and this grade stays out of the book. Or, continue as you've been doing. I can promise if you choose that option, though, that you'll wish you hadn't." She softened her tone slightly. "Jeff, I'm not insisting that you get all A's instantly. Just show me that you're *trying*. You can start by doing another composition under the instruction of your tutor."

Jeff unfolded the piece of paper and read the name. Beth Ledbetter. Below there was a phone number and an address. Jeff recognized them both.

Oh, great, Jeff thought to himself. This is Bucky's and Hayes's sister! Wonder how long it will take before word gets around the team and people start taking bets on whether I'll be thrown off again or not?

Out loud, he said, "Thanks, Ms. Collins. I'll — I'll call her right when I get home tonight. Right after hockey practice, I mean."

Ms. Collins smiled at him wearily. "Of course. But Jeff, keep in mind that sometimes good grades are more important than sports. You have to learn to train your mind as well as your body. I'll look forward to seeing a different, improved composition from you in two weeks. Okay, take your seat."

For the rest of class, Jeff tried to concentrate on what he was doing instead of on the call he had promised to make. But he kept drifting back to it and to what Ms. Collins had said before she told him to sit down.

Train your mind . . . where had he heard that before?

Midway through math class it dawned on him. Eric Stone had said the same thing in his letter. Jeff knew it was time to listen to what they were saying, but he couldn't help wishing it didn't mean getting tutored by his teammates' sister! He sighed.

"Yes, Mr. Connors? Are you experiencing

some hardship? Perhaps you'd like to share it with the rest of the class?" his math teacher asked drily.

Jeff shook his head. No way! he thought, as he turned his attention back to the problem on the board. I'd like anything *but* that!

At practice that afternoon, Jeff suited up right away and was one of the first players out on the ice. He skated around for a few seconds, just to get the feel of it, then came back to the bench when the coach blew his whistle.

After fifteen minutes of drills, Coach Wallace handed out red pinnies to half the players. Jeff was one of them. As he tied his pinny over his jersey, he listened to the coach explain that they were going to scrimmage for the rest of the practice. He wanted to see how certain combinations of players worked together.

Jeff lined up at right wing. Bucky took up position at center, with Hayes to his left. Looking over his shoulder, Jeff saw that Kevin was backing him up at right defense. Shep was at left defense. It took Jeff a moment to realize that the figure in the goal covered in pads and protective gear was Michael Gillis.

This could be the starting lineup, Jeff suddenly thought. His heart pounded. If I do well in this scrimmage, maybe I'll earn a permanent spot here.

Six other boys took up position on the other half of the ice. Jeff looked up to see Chad facing him.

"Are you ready to go down?" Chad whispered in his best menacing voice.

"You first," Jeff growled back. They grinned at each other and waited for the scrimmage to begin.

Coach Wallace dropped the puck for the

face-off. The red team took control. Jeff circled around until he reached the right zone. He caught Bucky's eye. Bucky's stick flashed and a moment later the puck hit Jeff's stick. Without looking down at it, he checked around him to see where his teammates were. Was anyone in the clear?

Hayes was. Jeff skated forward to close the space between them a bit more, then shot him a pass. Hayes fumbled it for a moment, then gained control. But that brief delay gave his defender enough time to close in.

Jeff could see Hayes was in trouble. He wanted to help out, but Chad was stuck on him like flypaper. Bucky shook free of his defender and Hayes sent him the puck. Bucky took it behind the net, quickly shifting the play to the opposite side of the ice.

Jeff was too far in the middle to receive a pass. But Kevin was clear. Bucky passed the puck to him, then skated nearer to the goal. Jeff saw Kevin glance at him, then at Bucky. To Jeff's disappointment, he returned the puck to Bucky. Bucky scooped it up and delivered a lightning-quick backhand shot. The goalie never saw it coming. Score!

As the teams skated back into position, Kevin said to Jeff, "I wanted to give you a chance, but that big lug Chad was barreling down on you from behind. I didn't think you saw him."

"I didn't!" replied Jeff. He took up his position opposite Chad. "But I will next time."

Chad waggled his eyebrows. "We'll see about that."

At the next face-off, the blue team made a strong effort to get the draw. It didn't do much good. The puck caught an edge and bounced crazily all over the ice. Every time a player came near it, the disk went off in another direction.

Finally, the blue team got the puck under its control. The center started to move in closer to the red goal.

"Pass it!" Coach Wallace yelled. "Move it around!"

The blue center hesitated for a moment. That was his mistake. Bucky swooped in and captured the puck. Hayes was already streaking over the center line and heading for the attacking zone.

But Bucky had been stopped in the defending zone by a double team of defensemen. He couldn't pass to Hayes without risking an offside call. Even though it was only a scrimmage, Jeff knew Bucky was too good a player to deliberately cause an offense. So, instead of sending the puck to his brother, he dropped a quick pass back to Shep.

Shep skated furiously into the neutral zone. By that time, Hayes had turned around and come back toward center ice. The two were close enough now for Shep to make a good pass.

Hayes collected the puck carefully and took off down the ice again. Bucky shook free of his defender and skated parallel to him. All Hayes had to do was pass the puck over and Bucky would have an easy shot at the goal.

From where Jeff was, it looked simple enough.

But somehow Hayes botched it. He sent the puck skyrocketing behind the net and around the board to the opposite side.

A blue defender pounced on it and sent it skimming down the ice. As the red team chased after it, Jeff heard Bucky hiss at Hayes, "Dummy!"

From the number of players who cast looks in that direction, Jeff knew that everyone else on the ice had heard it, too. Hayes turned bright red under his helmet but kept his eyes straight ahead.

For the rest of the scrimmage, Jeff could see that Hayes's heart wasn't in the game. Midway through, Coach Wallace made some team changes. He brought in some guys from the bench, switched blue players to red and vice versa, and pointed the leftovers to the sidelines. Chad took over for Hayes, Bucky stayed in center, and Kevin remained where he was. Jeff wound up on the bench next to Hayes.

When the shuffling around was finished, Jeff got a surprise when he saw who had replaced him. It was Sam Metcalf!

Guess Coach really meant what he said about alternates getting even playing time, Jeff thought.

He could tell right from the first face-off

that Sam was a solid team player. He, Chad, and Bucky made a powerful front line. Passes were sharp and accurate. Run after run down the ice, the threesome eluded their defenders to take shots on goal.

Fifteen minutes later, Coach Wallace mixed things up again. Jeff returned to right wing, but on the blue team, with Shep backing him up on defense. They performed well together, but Jeff still felt he and Kevin were the obvious duo.

Coach Wallace blew his whistle.

"Okay, one last change around, then we'll all cool down and head for the showers." When he had finished repositioning people, Jeff found himself on the bench sitting between Sam and Bucky. Hayes and Kevin were on the seats behind them.

"Boy, that felt great!" Sam said enthusiastically. Then his grin faded. "I gotta tell you guys, it's pretty hard sitting on the bench. I was a regular starter at my old school." He sighed.

Bucky shrugged. "Well, you never know. The reason Coach made those alternate positions is so he can dump some dead weight if he needs to — or if he *has* to. Right, Jeff?" He elbowed Jeff sharply in the ribs.

Jeff cut Bucky an angry look. "Or maybe he'll decide he wants to put a real team player, a guy who shows a good attitude toward his teammates, on the ice instead of some loudmouth who spends half his time criticizing other players!" he shot back.

"Well, I'm sure he'd rather have a loudmouth than a 'fraidy cat! Or should I say 'fraidy *dog?*" Bucky replied sarcastically.

Jeff felt his face turn beet red.

"Hey, you guys, break it up," Kevin whispered. "The coach is coming over."

The last scrimmage had ended and Coach Wallace was signaling the boys to skate a few laps, then head for the showers. As they made their way to the locker room, Jeff caught Hayes's arm.

"Listen, I just want you to know I thought you played well out there today."

Hayes stared at him. "What makes you think I don't think I did?" he asked.

"Come on, Hayes, I heard what Bucky said to you —"

"Will you quit worrying about me? I can handle Bucky. What I can't handle is some no-brain like you trying to mother me!"

He shook free of Jeff's grasp and ran into the locker room, leaving Jeff to stare after him in stunned silence.

10

Hayes's words were still ringing in Jeff's ears at dinner. It made what he had to do after dessert that much more difficult. But he knew he couldn't avoid it, no matter what.

So after he had helped clear the dishes, he grabbed the cordless phone and shut himself in the bathroom. He fished the slip of paper Ms. Collins had given him out of his pocket and dialed the number.

"Hello?" a female voice answered.

"Uh, hi, is Beth there?" Jeff asked.

"This is Beth."

"Oh. My name is Jeff Connors. Um, Ms.

Collins said you might tutor me in English."
He told her about his conversation with his teacher.

"Do you still have the composition you turned in?" Beth asked.

"Sure," he replied.

"Good," she said. "Sometimes people get so angry they tear them up. So we're off on the right foot already."

She sounded so nice that Jeff started to relax. Maybe this tutoring won't be so bad after all, he thought. If only it wasn't Bucky's and Hayes's sister!

"Bring your composition with you tomorrow and we'll get started," Beth said.

Jeff gulped. "So soon?" he asked. "I have hockey practice tomorrow, then I'll want to eat dinner. Couldn't we start this weekend? And couldn't you come over here?"

"No, I'm sorry, but I'm all set up here. And it really would be better to get you going sooner rather than later. It will only be for an hour. So how about it?"

Jeff sighed, knowing she was right. "Let me check with my folks, okay?" He got permission from both his mother and father, then told Beth he'd be at her house at 7:30 sharp. I only hope the Ledbetter brothers aren't around, he thought dismally. But what are the chances of that?

School flew by the next day. Jeff told Ms. Collins he was going to be seeing Beth that very night. She looked so pleased that he was glad he hadn't put off his first tutoring session.

At practice, he concentrated on playing well. He was rewarded by being teamed up with other players he knew would be selected for the first string. Happily, Kevin was in the defenseman slot behind him more often than not.

When the session was over, Coach Wallace announced that they would be playing a non-league game on Saturday afternoon. The starting lineup would be posted Friday before practice.

Whose names would appear on that list was all any of the guys could talk about. Heated discussions about who had seen the most playing time during practice, who played well with whom, and why certain combinations of front line and defense made the most sense took up all the conversation in the locker room.

"Listen, there's no way he's going to put Shep Fredrickson and Jordan Owens together on defense," argued Chad. "They both play the left side of the ice better than the right! One's going to be a starter, the other will sub in."

Shep said, "Kevin, you and Jeff make a good front line/defenseman team. I'll bet you guys start out on the right wing and defense slots."

Only Michael Gillis seemed sure of his place on the team. He was a safe bet for the starting goalie slot and everyone knew it.

Though he listened carefully, Jeff didn't take part in the conversation. He was too busy wondering what his first tutoring session was going to be like.

Jeff and Kevin walked home together as usual, but for some reason Jeff didn't feel like telling Kevin what he was doing later that night.

He'll find out soon enough, he thought ruefully. If Bucky sees me, I'm sure he'll let the whole team know.

At dinner, Jeff ate as if he'd never seen food before, then gathered together everything he thought he might need for his meeting: his three-ring binder, his composi-

67

tion, a pencil, and a pen. His mother drove him to the Ledbetters' house, promising to be back in an hour. She handed him an envelope with Beth's name on the outside and a check on the inside, then drove away.

Jeff walked to the front door and rang the bell. Hayes answered it.

"Jeff! What're you doing here?" Hayes asked, looking surprised.

"Uh, I'm here to see your sister," Jeff mumbled.

Hayes stepped aside. "Come on in," he said.

"Is that Jeff Connors?" a voice called out.

Blushing furiously, Jeff pushed past Hayes just as Beth came into the room. While they shook hands, Hayes muttered something about going to his room and disappeared.

Jeff liked Beth immediately. About the same age as his sister Candy, she was dressed in sweats and running shoes. Her blond hair was cut short and her blue eyes were sizing him up just as he was sizing her up.

"Come on into my study," she said. "And let's see what you've brought me."

"Oh, uh, here," Jeff said, fumbling with the envelope his mother had given him.

Beth laughed. "I meant let's take a look at your composition, but since you're offering . . ." She whisked the envelope out of his hand and stowed it quickly in the top drawer of her desk.

"Now let me see the famous composition, the one with all the green marks," she said with a smile.

"Oh, boy, here we go," said Jeff.

"Don't worry," said Beth. "Believe me, the worst part is just getting here, and that's over and done with."

Jeff looked at her with raised eyebrows. "How'd you know that?" he asked.

"Hey, I was once in your shoes myself,"

she said. "Everyone goes through a slow patch in school. Only some of us get down to a crawl and need a little help to get back on track. I'm here to help you do that."

She read through the composition. Then she pulled out an expensive-looking binder. She flipped it open to a blank page and jotted down some notes.

"Okay, here's what I see you doing wrong," she said matter-of-factly. "You write incomplete sentences, for one thing. You know, missing a verb or a noun or something important like that. You also switch tenses in mid-sentence and mid-paragraph. You'll be talking in past tense one minute, then suddenly we're in present tense! Without the right tense, your work won't make sense."

"You're a poet and don't know it?" Jeff asked with a smile, referring to her little rhyme.

"Believe it or not, it's things like that that

70

will help you remember what to watch for. I'll teach you a whole ton of stupid sayings like that, and you'll never be able to get them out of your head. Like that old 'i before e except after c' one."

Jeff grinned. "I see what you mean. So, what else is wrong?"

Beth listed a few other problems she'd noticed. When she was through, Jeff felt a little overwhelmed and told her so.

Beth punched him lightly on the arm. "Hey, you don't have to tackle it all at once. That's why I'm here — to help make things clear."

Jeff tried to keep a straight face but burst out laughing. "Is becoming a poet part of the bargain?"

Beth laughed with him, then said, "Just keep that attitude and you'll be writing sonnets in no time. Now let's get to work."

11

The remainder of Jeff's week was filled with classes, practices, and tutoring sessions. His meetings with Beth were getting a little easier, though the first time he ran into Bucky, he was embarrassed. Bucky had razzed him about the tutoring until Beth told him to lay off. Since then, Bucky had given him a nasty smile but said nothing.

Despite this, Jeff fell into bed each night tired but satisfied that he was doing everything he could to stay on track in school and in hockey.

When classes let out on Friday, the members of the Winston Blades hockey team raced to the rink. As promised, the roster was posted. It read this way:

Center — B. Ledbetter
Right Wing — J. Connors
Left Wing — C. Galbraith
Right Defense — K. Leach
Left Defense — S. Fredrickson
Goal — M. Gillis

Jeff and Kevin slapped each other a high five, then hurried to change for practice. On the way, Kevin whispered, "I'm glad the coach finally decided to pair Chad up with Shep at left wing and left defense. Chad and I worked okay together at right when you were on the bench — better than Hayes and Shep did at left! — but I think Chad and Shep are a real power team, don't you?"

Jeff nodded. "I was a little worried yesterday that Coach was going to play Hayes at right instead of me."

Kevin shrugged. "Nah, you and I are too good together. Besides, I'm sure Coach'll sub him in, just like he does during practice. He likes to play everybody during these non-league games. Gives him a chance to see who might crack under pressure!"

As they wrestled into their gear and laced up their skates, one last thought occurred to Jeff. "Do you think Coach'll sub in the alternates tomorrow, too? I'd sure like to see how Sam Metcalf does during a game."

"Better be careful what you wish for, pal. If Sam comes in, you may find yourself warming the bench!" Kevin teased.

Jeff laughed. "Good point! Forget I said anything!"

The two skated onto the ice for the warm-up. Before the practice began, Coach Wallace gathered the team together for a pep talk. "Okay, Blades, listen up! Today we practice long and hard. Tonight you sleep long and hard. Tomorrow you eat a good breakfast and lunch and show up here raring to go! I'll want to see fire in your eyes, sparks flying from your skates, and every player looking sharp and ready! Be here by two so we can get in a warm-up before the game starts. Any questions?"

A loud chorus of no's rang across the rink.

"Well then, what are you waiting for?" Coach Wallace roared. "Get on that ice and give me three lines!"

The boys clambered on and took their positions. Jeff could see that everyone was gung ho to do his best. He felt pride in his team and in himself for being a part of it.

Best of all, it didn't seem as though any of the others had heard of his tutoring sessions.

Guess Bucky decided not to say anything, he thought. And that's just fine with me!

12

Bright and early Saturday morning, Jeff checked his duffel bag to make sure he had all his hockey equipment. He had an appointment with Beth and planned to go to the game immediately afterward.

It had been Beth's suggestion that he try writing his make-up composition before the game. "That way, when you win, you'll be able to celebrate instead of having to do this assignment," she said. It made sense to Jeff, so, after a hearty breakfast of pancakes and sausage, he hurried over to the Ledbetter house, ready to get the job done before he headed for the rink.

Beth showed him into the study. Jeff reached into his duffel for his notebook, then slapped his hand to his head.

"I forgot to bring paper!" he moaned. Beth laughed.

"What kind of tutor would I be if I didn't have paper?" she asked. She pulled out her binder and opened it. Jeff noticed again how expensive it looked. Beth caught his look.

"My dad got it for me," she explained, showing him her initials embossed on the front. "All three of us Ledbetter kids have one."

Jeff saw for the first time that the binder was a two-ring. Beth pulled the rings apart and handed him some notebook paper. She told him to start writing his make-up composition and said that she would check on him in half an hour.

Left to himself, Jeff's mind went blank. He just couldn't think of a thing to write. Instead, he fiddled with the two big rings on Beth's notebook. He pulled them open and snapped them shut, open and shut.

This is ridiculous, he thought. Coming up with a subject should be the easy part, right?

Yeah, right.

He got up and shook out his arms and legs. He could see heavy gray clouds drifting by the study window. As he stared out, he saw Kevin come down the street leading Ranger on a long leash. The black dog frolicked about, barking and sniffing everything in sight. Kevin grinned at Ranger and ruffled his fur.

That's it! Jeff suddenly thought. I'll write about Kevin and Ranger!

He made it through the first paragraph.

Then he ran out of things to say. After sitting for five minutes, staring at the half-empty paper, he suddenly thought of a better topic. He tore the paper in half, tossed it into the trash can, and started again.

This time, he wrote about Eric Stone's letter and how it had helped him decide to try working with a tutor.

When Beth knocked softly on the door, he was ready.

Beth settled herself in an armchair. "So, what did you decide to write about?" she asked.

"Well, I started writing about my friend Kevin and his dog, Ranger. I'm not a big fan of dogs, but I want to try to like this one since it belongs to my best friend. But I didn't get very far, so I decided to write about my favorite hockey player and a letter I got from him."

Just then, the doorbell rang. Beth moved

to answer it, but before she had risen from the chair, Bucky walked by the study door.

"You guys keep working, I'll get that," he said.

Beth looked startled, then puzzled. "I thought he was up in his room," she said. "Oh, well, he must have been on his way to the kitchen or something. Anyway, mind if I take a look at the paper?"

Jeff handed it over. "You've written a lot there," she observed. "Now let's see how you've done."

Beth's usual way of correcting his papers was to circle his errors in red. Then they worked together to figure out how to correct them.

But when she handed him back his paper this time, he saw there were only red check marks in the margins on the side of the paper.

"I've indicated the lines where the errors

are," she explained. "Now it's up to you to find them and fix them."

"But I'm the one who made the mistakes in the first place!" Jeff said. "How do I find them?"

"You've been training yourself all week to construct sentences that make sense. Be a detective and sniff out the clues!"

Jeff focused his attention on the sheet of paper and stared at the first check mark. Then his eyes slid across the line to the sentence. After a moment, his eyes lit up.

"I see it!" he said triumphantly. Before long, he had found the rest of the mistakes as well. He and Beth talked them over and she agreed that he had identified them all.

"Now all that's left is for you to copy the composition over on a clean sheet of paper and hand it in on Monday," Beth said with a smile.

Jeff nodded. He was still nervous about

his writing, but he accepted a fresh piece of paper from her special binder. Slowly, carefully, he rewrote the composition. When he was done, Beth pronounced it perfect. "But I don't think you have time to listen to my praises. Don't you have to be somewhere?"

Jeff looked at the clock. It was 1:40! "Yikes! I'm supposed to be at warm-ups in twenty minutes!" He gathered up the two papers, shoved them into his duffel bag, and ran for the door. Just before he left, he called out, "Thanks, Beth!"

She grinned and replied, "Just make sure that paper gets to Ms. Collins in one piece!"

13

Jeff ran all the way to the rink. He was panting like a dog on a hot afternoon when he burst into the locker room.

"Whoa, where's the fire?" Kevin asked jokingly.

"I lost track of time!" Jeff said, gasping for breath. A moment later, Hayes Ledbetter came hurrying in.

"Hayes! I thought you'd come over with Bucky. I would have waited for you," Jeff said.

"That's okay," Hayes said. "Bucky came

early. I had some things I had to do. Guess I lost track of time."

"Sure sign of a real professional," a voice behind them said. It was Bucky. "What were you doing, playing computer games?"

"It was a — an extra-credit writing exercise," Hayes mumbled. Bucky rolled his eyes and snorted.

Jeff felt sorry for Hayes and wished his brother would lay off him for one minute. But he didn't say anything because he knew it was none of his business.

He headed for the ice the minute he was suited up. Several other players, including members of the other team, were already warming up. Jeff waved hello to Chad, Shep, and Sam, then concentrated on preparing himself for the game. When the whistle blew, he was raring to go.

Coach Wallace called them all together. "Okay, Blades, this may not be for the record, but think of how great you'll feel to have a real win under your belts! So go out there and do your stuff!"

The boys cheered. The starting lineup took their positions. Jeff glanced back at Kevin, who gave him an excited thumbs-up.

Bucky and the center for the Clover Rovers readied themselves for the face-off. When the referee dropped the puck, they scrambled frantically. Bucky came out the winner.

He slammed a pass to Chad almost immediately. Chad controlled it and headed down the ice. A defenseman was on him like glue. With a swift flick of the wrist, Chad passed the puck back to Bucky.

Jeff followed the action closely, looking for a chance to help out. When Bucky received the pass, Jeff faked out his defenseman and skated free.

"C'mon, Bucky, give it up! I'm in the

clear!" he muttered to himself. As if he had heard him, Bucky sent the puck skimming over the ice toward his right wing.

Jeff reached the puck, but a second later he was slammed into the boards by an out-of-control Rover defenseman. No foul was called. With a grunt, he pushed himself off. The puck skittered away from him. But to his relief, he saw Kevin snatch it up.

Kevin skated slowly toward the middle, apparently looking to pass to either Bucky or Chad. But Jeff knew better. Kevin was preparing for a play they had perfected in the past week. All the Blades knew what was coming, but Jeff counted on the Rovers' being fooled.

They were. When Kevin turned quickly and passed the puck to Jeff, Jeff was practically standing by himself. He skated with fast, slashing moves right toward the goal. But at the last second, he slipped behind the net and ricocheted the puck against the boards.

Chad was already on his way to meet it. Like a well-oiled machine, his stick found the puck. All he had to do was backhand it into the goal. And that's just what he did.

Cheers roared up from the Blades' bench and the few fans who had come out to watch the non-league event. Jeff beamed, knowing that the scorekeeper was putting a nice fat check mark down in the assist column beside his name.

Back at center ice, Bucky and the Rover center were ready for the next face-off. This time, the Rover won. He made a beeline pass to his right wing. The wing treated it like a hot potato, wasting no time in sending it right on back.

Shep was too quick for him, however. He sneaked in and stole the puck in mid-pass. One swift move later and Chad had control.

But not for long — he tapped the puck just a little too hard and sent it skimming beyond his reach. A Rover defenseman picked it up and gave it a hearty whack.

It had all happened so quickly, the rest of the Rovers were caught off guard. The puck whizzed by them despite their desperate lunges to stop it. Kevin nabbed it and moved behind the Blades' net. When he emerged on the opposite side, Shep was waiting. Kevin passed off, and Shep kept the puck going, this time sending it to Bucky.

Bucky stickhandled the disk straight down the center of the ice. As Jeff skated to stay parallel with him, he knew his efforts were wasted. Bucky was going to drive in and shoot the puck right down the goalie's throat if he could.

He could. Bucky pulled up short with an ice-flying stop and, with a move so quick it was difficult to follow, launched the puck into the air. It soared past the goalie's out-stretched glove and into the net for the second goal of the game.

Coach Wallace took advantage of the break in action to put in some subs. Chad and Jeff both came out, as did Shep. With a slight twinge of jealousy, Jeff noted that Hayes had replaced him at right wing. He told himself not to be greedy, however, and grabbed a seat next to Sam Metcalf.

Sam offered him a cup of water. Jeff drank it gratefully. Then he watched the game and shouted encouragement with the rest of the bench.

"Sure hope I get out there sometime today," Sam said at one point.

Jeff felt sorry for him. He knew only too well what it was like to want to play. Of course, Sam stood a very good chance of seeing ice time — unlike Jeff the year before.

Well, that's not going to happen this year, not with that composition I've got sitting in my duffel bag, he thought with determination.

Sam did get a chance to play later in the game. Coach put him in at right wing after he took Hayes out. Sam impressed everybody on the team with his sharp passes, speedy skating, and aggressive play. He even assisted on the Blades' third goal of the day.

"Looks like you and I are neck and neck for assists!" he commented when Jeff came in to replace him. Jeff grinned back.

"We'll see if I can't change that!" he called.

But three goals were all the Blades would score that game. It was enough to give them the win. And as Coach Wallace had predicted, even though it wasn't for the record, it felt good.

The mood in the locker room was jubilant. Jeff and some of the other boys even sang victory songs while they showered.

Towel around his waist and still singing, Jeff left the shower area to get dressed. When he turned the corner to his row of lockers, he stopped abruptly. His locker was wide open and a figure was crouched in front of it. Jeff could see that the person's hand was on the zipper of his duffel bag.

"Hey!" Jeff yelped.

The figure spun around. It was Sam Metcalf!

"What are you doing?" Jeff asked, his surprise clearly showing on his face.

Sam looked puzzled. "What do you mean? I'm getting my stuff together!"

"You're getting *my* stuff together, you mean," Jeff corrected him. "That's my locker and my duffel bag!"

Sam let go of the duffel as if it were on fire. Then he peered up at the number on the locker door.

"Number 207, whoops," he said. "I thought this was number 107." He hurried over to the next row and came back carrying a duffel. Except for the fact that the handles on Jeff's bag were gold while Sam's were white, the two bags were identical. "See why I got confused?"

Jeff laughed. "Yeah, no problem," he said. "But I think I'll count my socks just to make sure there are still two of them in here. Can't be too careful, you know!"

Sam laughed, too, then disappeared back into his own row of lockers. Jeff heard him humming the victory song.

14

Jeff loafed around for the rest of the weekend, enjoying the fact that his homework was already done. When Monday morning came, he set off for school with a light heart. His composition was tucked neatly in his notebook. For once, he was looking forward to English class.

But Ms. Collins wasn't in class that day. A short, gray-haired man with wire-rimmed glasses was sitting behind her desk when Jeff arrived.

"Ms. Collins is away at a teachers' conference. I'm substituting for the week," explained the stranger.

"Oh, I have this composition to turn in," said Jeff. "Maybe I could leave it on her desk?"

"Fine," said the substitute. "I'll add a little note to document when it was turned in. Just put it down there."

Jeff did, then took his seat.

"Guess we'll soon see how good a tutor my sister is, huh?" whispered Hayes across the aisle.

Jeff nodded. He didn't want to admit it, but he was a little disappointed Ms. Collins wasn't there to read the composition right away. Then he smiled to himself.

Who would have thought I'd be anxious for someone to read something I'd written? he thought. As he listened to the substitute drone on, he found himself wishing for another reason that Ms. Collins were there —

at least she made the material sound inter-esting!

At practice that afternoon, Coach Wallace sat the Blades down on the benches. He praised them for their solid victory against the Clover Rovers. He was pointing out some of their mistakes when the sound of a door slamming made him stop.

Jeff turned with the rest of the team to see who was causing the commotion. It was Hayes Ledbetter.

"Nice of you to join us, Hayes," the coach said sarcastically. Hayes mumbled some-thing about being tied up with a teacher un-expectedly.

The rest of practice was uneventful. The only exciting thing that happened was that Coach Wallace handed out the game sched-ule. Their first league game was to take place on Saturday.

Jeff and Kevin talked about the practice and the upcoming game the whole walk home. They were only interrupted when Kevin's helmet fell out of his duffel bag.

"How'd that zipper get unzipped?" Kevin wondered. "I was sure I'd closed it tight."

"Maybe it's broken," Jeff replied.

Kevin grimaced. "If it is, I'll be in big trouble. This bag is practically brand new!"

"Here, let me see it," Jeff said. He took the helmet from Kevin, shoved it into the bag, then fiddled with the zipper for a moment until it worked again. "There you go. Nothing I wouldn't do to keep you out of trouble!"

They parted laughing. Jeff hurried the rest of the way home, hungry for dinner.

He ate two helpings of spaghetti and three rolls. "No room for salad," he said when his mother urged him to eat "some kind of green thing." But he managed to polish off a bowl of ice cream ten minutes later.

"Okay, mister, time to earn your keep. Those recycling bins aren't going to wait any longer," his father said when the dishes had been cleared.

Jeff groaned, but heaved himself up. He knew it wouldn't take long to finish his chore. Then he could sack out on the couch for a while.

Mr. Connors had built a number of collection bins onto the side of the garage. Jeff's job was to separate the material for recycling and the bottles and cans to be returned to the market from the rubbish. Once a month, he joined his father on the trip to the recycling center, where they turned in all that they had collected. Jeff's father paid him ten dollars each trip, so Jeff couldn't really complain.

He had just brought out a stack of maga-

97

zines that he'd tied up with a piece of string when he heard someone whistling a tune out in front of the house. He looked down the driveway and saw Kevin passing by with Ranger on his usual long leash.

Jeff watched them for a moment or two. Ranger really did seem like a well-behaved, friendly dog. And he was on a leash. Jeff decided now was as good a time as any to try to learn to like Ranger.

"Hey, Kev, how are you and the dog doing?" he called out as he walked toward them.

Kevin's head snapped around. "A fat lot you care! You'd probably be happy if my dog dropped dead right in front of you, wouldn't you! Come on, Ranger, let's get out of here!"

Jeff was stunned. Instinctively, he ran down the driveway after them.

He was too late. The darkness of the night had swallowed them up. Before long, he couldn't even hear the sound of their footsteps. But Kevin's words continued to resound in his ears, loud and clear.

As soon as Jeff got back to the house, he picked up the telephone and called Kevin.

The line was busy.

He tried again five minutes later. This time the call went through.

"Hi, Mrs. Leach? This is Jeff. Is Kevin there?" he asked. He heard her muffle the phone and call out for Kevin. Then she got back on the line.

"Kevin's doing his homework right now, Jeff. He can't come to the phone."

"Oh," said Jeff. "Well, could you tell

him . . . tell him that I called? Thanks." He hung up the phone.

I'll corner him at school tomorrow, he promised himself, and find out what the heck this is all about!

The next morning Jeff arrived at school earlier than usual. He found his way to Kevin's locker and waited for him to show up.

Kids came by, opened their lockers, put away their coats, took out books. But no Kevin.

Wonder if he's home sick? Jeff thought.

Yet on his way to class, he spotted Kevin at the end of a long corridor. He was coming out of the administrative office.

Late, I guess, Jeff figured. He was just late, that's all.

The two boys had one class together: history. Jeff was sure Kevin wouldn't miss that. He decided to talk to him there.

But when he arrived, Kevin was up at the front of the room talking to Mr. Leone, their teacher. Jeff moved up closer, but there was no way he could interrupt their conversation. Finally, everyone but the two boys was seated.

"Whatever it is, Jeff, it'll have to wait until after class. Take your seats, please, boys," said Mr. Leone.

Frustrated, Jeff moved to his desk. Kevin's chair was across the room, so he didn't stand a chance of talking to him all period.

When the bell rang, Kevin was off like a flash. But Jeff was in hot pursuit.

"Just a minute, Jeffrey. Wasn't there something you wanted to talk to me about?" Mr. Leone asked. Jeff slowed down long enough to say he'd figured it out on his own. But by the time he'd reached the hallway, Kevin was nowhere to be seen.

For the rest of the day, even at lunch, Kevin eluded him. It was only when they gathered for hockey practice that Jeff had his chance to confront him.

Even then, Jeff could tell it wasn't going to do any good.

"Will you just tell me if I heard you right last night?" Jeff demanded.

Kevin simply stared at the floor and shook his head. He laced on his skates furiously and stomped on his runners out of the locker room without a word.

Jeff decided the only thing he could do was wait for Kevin to talk to him. For now, he'd just go through practice as usual.

But practice was anything but usual. Every time Coach Wallace teamed Jeff and Kevin up on the right side, Jeff felt as though he were playing with someone he'd never met before.

"I'll bet you didn't connect on one pass the whole time you were out there," said Coach Wallace to the two of them when they were on the bench. "I suppose it had to happen sometime. I just hope that it's not a permanent situation. I'd hate to have to re-think my starting lineup again. But maybe I'll have to do just that."

Jeff's face didn't show it, but his heart sank. He had tried so hard to earn his place on the team. He decided then and there that he wasn't going to let some attitude of Kevin's blow it for him.

When practice was over, Jeff was all set to make a beeline for Kevin. He was going to get to the bottom of things right away!

But on the way to the locker room, Bucky grabbed his arm. Jeff struggled to shake him loose, but Bucky held him tighter. "Listen," he said. "Keep away from Kevin in there. I'll talk to you after he's gone."

Jeff looked at Bucky with surprise and nodded. Maybe Bucky knew something about it. It was worth checking out, anyway.

When the locker room had cleared out, Bucky came over and sat next to Jeff.

"All I can tell you is that you'd better back off for a while," he said. "Kevin hasn't said much except that he's really steamed about your note."

"My note? What note?" Jeff demanded. "I don't know anything about any note. What's he talking about?"

"Search me," Bucky said with a shrug. "I'm telling you everything I know. And giving you my advice to stay away from him until he cools down."

But Jeff just couldn't leave it that way. He'd gone a whole day without speaking to his best friend. He was determined that the next day would be different.

That night after dinner, he got permission

to go to Kevin's house. Instead of going around back as he usually did, he rang the front doorbell. He didn't want to give Kevin a chance to hole up.

Kevin answered the door. Ranger was right behind him, swishing his tail and barking.

"Quiet, Ranger," Kevin said. Then he looked at Jeff. "What do *you* want?"

Jeff drew a deep breath. The sight of Ranger had shaken him, but he knew he had to get by the dog in order to talk to Kevin. So, while Kevin stood with his hand on the doorknob, Jeff barged right in and headed for Kevin's room.

"Hey! Wait a minute!" Kevin called. "Ranger, come on!" He followed Jeff into his room and demanded, "What do you think you're doing?"

Jeff shut the door. "I don't want anyone to interrupt us."

Kevin hugged Ranger protectively. "If you lay one finger on my dog —"

"Why would you say something dumb like that?" Jeff asked, shocked.

"Why? Because you said yourself that if you ever got the chance, you'd see what you could do to get rid of him. Well, I'm not going to give you that chance!"

"I never said anything like that!"

"Did too! You even put it in writing!" Kevin jumped up, tore open his desk drawer, and shoved a piece of paper in Jeff's hands. "Just try to deny it now!"

Jeff unfolded the paper and read:

There may be a lot of nice dogs in this world, but some are just plain mean. Kevin's dog Ranger is one of those. I don't know why Kevin spends so much time with him since he's such a dumb dog. In fact, he'd be better

off if he had Ranger put away so that he didn't
waste any more time on that rotten mutt.

Though there was something slightly familiar about it, Jeff knew he'd never written that paragraph. He'd never written — or said — anything so awful.

Yet the handwriting looked just like his! Before he had a chance to examine it closely, however, Kevin had snatched it away from him.

"You're pretty quiet all of a sudden," Kevin said accusingly.

"Kevin, I didn't —"

"I know what your handwriting looks like."

"But I never wrote that!" Jeff shouted. "Where did it come from? Where did you find it?"

"You know I found it in my duffel bag last night. I bet you put it there when you pretended to fix my zipper!"

Jeff shook his head. "But Kevin, why would I want to write something like that?"

"Who knows?" Kevin said, avoiding his eyes. "All I know is what I know. And I know that you don't like dogs and that that's your handwriting on that piece of paper. So if you didn't write it, tell me who did." He walked to his door and opened it. "If you can't tell me that, then we have nothing to say to each other."

The next day, Jeff had only one thing on his mind: to find out who had played such a dirty trick on him and his best buddy. But no matter how much he puzzled over it, he couldn't figure out who would do such a rotten thing. Or why.

He and Kevin played no better together than they had at Tuesday's practice. Jeff had never realized before what a difference good communication between teammates made. Now he felt the effects of bad communication every minute he was on the ice.

It was the same thing on Thursday. Kevin

avoided him at school and didn't talk to him at all at practice. The other Blades were starting to notice. Jeff saw Sam Metcalf talking to Kevin. The two glanced over at him and Kevin shook his head. Though he couldn't hear what they were saying, Jeff was sure they were talking about him.

By the time Friday afternoon rolled around, Jeff was sure he wasn't going to be seeing his name on the starting lineup roster.

But he was wrong. When the list went up, he saw that Coach Wallace had stayed with the same six players. He could only hope that Kevin would put aside his anger by game time Saturday.

If only I could figure out who the saboteur is! Kevin thought desperately. It seemed hopeless.

Jeff and Beth Ledbetter had continued to meet off and on throughout the week. On

Friday afternoon, Beth said Jeff seemed to be getting the hang of it, but that he should still consider coming by for his Saturday-morning session. Jeff agreed. Now that he knew he was still in the starting lineup, he didn't dare risk letting his grades slip!

"By the way," Beth asked. "What did Ms. Collins think of your composition?"

"She hasn't been around to read it yet," Jeff said.

"Well, I hope it's in a safe place. It'd stink if all your hard work wound up missing or damaged!"

Saturday morning, Jeff awoke to see snow falling outside his window. He could smell scrambled eggs and English muffins cooking in the kitchen. With a contented sigh, he rolled out of bed to start his day.

Half an hour later, his mother dropped him off at the Ledbetters' house. He and Beth worked together for an hour and a half. Then it was time to get ready for his game. He had left his duffel bag in the car, so when his mother picked him up, they were set to head straight for the rink.

Jeff hopped out of the car, promising to make a goal for his mom. In the locker room, he dressed quickly, slipped on his skate guards, and hurried out to the rink.

As usual, a feeling of anticipation hit him the minute his skates touched the ice. The thrill of competition ahead always gave him a rush. He loved it all — the feel of the ice beneath him, the bright lights, the cold air on his face as he skated on the shimmering surface. He had to control his impulse to pour on the speed. He knew it would be better to save his strength for the game ahead.

And then he heard a familiar voice near the water jug.

"Are there any cups?" Kevin asked.

Within seconds, Jeff's happy mood was replaced by uneasiness. How will Kevin and I do on the ice together today? he wondered. We have to play better than we did this week.

But even as he thought it, he had a bad feeling that things weren't going to go well.

Minutes later, the rink was filled with skaters from both teams warming up. The Fremont Penguins were in solid blue with white numbers. They made a nice contrast to the Winston Blades' yellow uniforms.

Finally, the whistle blew and the two teams separated to their respective benches.

"Okay, let me have your attention," said Coach Wallace. "I want to see some heads-up hockey out there. Quick passes, sharp and accurate. Keep your eye on your positions. Talk to one another and set up the plays we've been working on all week. We're only a good team when we play like a team."

Jeff caught Kevin's eye for a brief second. Then Kevin looked away.

I hear you, Coach, Jeff thought. I hope Kevin does, too.

Coach Wallace interrupted his thoughts by yelling that it was time to take to the ice. Jeff shook his head, determined to stop puzzling over his problem until after the game. Instead, he skated onto the ice with the other Blades and prepared himself for the face-off.

The whistle blew. The puck dropped and the two centers scrambled to get their sticks around it.

The puck skittered on its edge past Jeff, rolled onto its side, and slid across the ice toward a player in blue and white. The Penguins took charge, dribbled it past the red middle line, and headed toward the Blades' goal.

The action skipped from one side of the

115

net to the other. But the puck never went in. Kevin finally managed to grab it after two good saves by Michael Gillis.

"Kevin! Kevin!" Jeff shouted. He was near the blue line, ready for a pass.

Kevin ignored him. Instead, he passed the puck to Chad, who dribbled it across the blue line. Bucky caught a pass from Chad and brought it across the midline into goal-scoring territory.

Jeff tried to get himself into a good scoring position. He waited for a pass, hoping that Bucky would put into action a play he, Jeff, and Kevin had had good luck with in the past. Before the note, that was.

Darn that note! Jeff thought angrily. It really messed things up!

As he thought about it, he felt something hit his skate.

The puck! He had let his mind wander only for a moment, but that had been long enough for him to miss out on making the play work. He tried to control the disk, but it ricocheted off his blade and slid back to the blue line.

Luckily for the Blades, Kevin was there. He trapped it with his stick, dribbled it into position, and slammed it toward the center. Bucky was right there. He caught the puck, spun around, and hit it with a forehand shot that went streaking at the net — and in!

Goal!

The Blades cheered and waved their sticks in the air as they congratulated Bucky and Kevin. The Penguins called for a time-out.

Clustered around their own bench, the Blades gave Coach Wallace their full attention.

"That goal was deserved," he said, "but it's time to start setting up some plays out there. Keep moving that puck and then take your best shot." The referee blew the whistle.

"One second, Jeff. You, too, Shep. Hayes, I want you to go in for Jeff. Jordan, you go in for Shep. Boys, grab some pine here."

Jeff's heart sank. He'd been in the game just five minutes. He took a seat behind Sam Metcalf without a word. Shep plunked down next to Sam.

Sam nudged Shep. "Hey, at least you're wearing a uniform," he said quietly. "I'd do just about anything to get on the squad. I'm likely to be sitting here all season in plain clothes unless . . ."

Jeff's ears perked up. He waited for Sam to finish his sentence. When Sam didn't, Jeff silently finished it for him.

Unless someone on the team has to give up his uniform.

17

Jeff tried to concentrate on the game. But he couldn't stop thinking about Sam. If Sam thought breaking up a good combination on the ice — a combination like Jeff and Kevin had been before the note turned up — would help his chances of getting on the team, would he try to do it?

Sitting behind Sam and listening to him cheer on the Blades, Jeff just couldn't believe he was capable of such a thing. He couldn't believe it, but couldn't deny that such a motive could have led to the note.

With a sigh, he turned his attention fully on the game.

The Penguins had taken control of the puck after the face-off. This time they weren't about to give up easily. The game got a lot more physical. First a two-minute penalty for high-sticking was called on the Penguins. Then Bucky was caught elbowing an opponent. Since the penalties left both teams short a man, neither converted them into a power-play advantage.

After several more minutes of back-and-forth shots on goal with no scoring, the first period ended. Coach Wallace had Jeff go back in for Hayes, with a caution to keep his eyes open and let his teammates know his position at all times.

Jeff was rested from his time on the bench and ready to play hard. The face-off went to the Blades. Jeff worked to get free for a pass. His first thought was to set up one of the plays with Kevin that worked so well. But before he could make another move, someone crashed into him from the side.

A burly Penguin defenseman sent him reeling toward the boards. Frantically, Jeff struggled to regain his balance. But at the last minute, his skates flew out from under him and he sprawled onto the ice.

As the referee's whistle blew, Jeff felt a spray of ice in his face. A player had skidded to a stop just shy of his prone body.

"Here!" a gruff voice said. It was Kevin, holding out a hand. "Come on! We've got just two minutes to put together a power play!"

Jeff grabbed the hand and scrambled to his feet. "Thanks," he said. But Kevin had skated off already.

For the next two minutes, the Blades tried to make the power play work. As the penalty time ticked down, it seemed they wouldn't be successful. Even though the Penguins were down a man, they had everyone covered.

Then Kevin got control. With a quick glance up, he sent the puck skimming toward Jeff. Jeff stopped it. Seeing that he was clear, he skated furiously in the direction of the Penguins' goal.

Closer. Closer. He shuffled the puck back and forth with the tip of his stick. Chad raced parallel with him down the ice. At the last possible second, Jeff flicked the disk across to the left wing. Chad simply let it ricochet off his stick toward the goal.

The Penguins goalkeeper lunged for it. But he was too late. The puck hit the back of the net — and the Blades were up 2–0!

Jeff and Chad slapped high fives and cheered. Jeff looked for Kevin to thank him for feeding him the puck. But when he caught his eye, Kevin just jerked his head up in acknowledgment and skated away.

Well, it's not much, but at least he's thawing a little, Jeff said to himself.

The Blades set up for the face-off. Jeff and the rest of the players tried their hardest to sweeten the lead. It was no use. The Penguins played by the book, sticking to their men like sand on a wet foot, stealing the puck every chance they could, and passing with finesse. By the end of the second period, they had inched up on the Blades with two goals of their own.

"You can take these guys," Coach Wallace assured them at a break. "Let's see some energy out there!"

But those two Penguin goals had dulled the Blades' sharpness. There was no spark. There was no extra push. And most noticeably, there were no words of encouragement on-ice. In fact, there was the exact opposite.

"C'mon, Chad, I'm way ahead of you!"

Bucky Ledbetter yelled after his left wing passed the puck too far behind him.

"Shep, where's the backup? Where's the backup?" Chad cried when Shep failed to pick up a pass that had skimmed under Chad's stick.

"Can't see! Can't see!" Michael Gillis called frantically when a pile of players landed in a heap near the goal.

Only Jeff and Kevin were silent.

When the buzzer ended the last period, Jeff had had it. He couldn't have cared less that their first game had concluded in a tie. All he wanted to do was shower up, walk home, and sit in the peace and quiet of his bedroom.

Most of all, he wanted to stop thinking about dogs, mean notes, and friendships gone sour.

18

Two days later, a dark cloud still hung over Jeff's head. He struggled through his morning classes. At lunchtime, he sat with the rest of the hockey team but didn't say a word. When he was through eating, he mumbled something about having to go to the library at free time afterward.

This day just can't get any worse, he thought as he crouched among the racks of books, pretending to read a biography on a famous hockey player.

But it did. Ms. Collins was back in class — and she wasn't happy. She handed him his make-up composition with a shake of her head.

As soon as he looked at it, he knew why she was upset. It was covered with green correction marks. There was no way he could have received a passing grade.

She must think I didn't even try! Jeff thought dismally.

Then the full magnitude of the situation hit him. If he didn't get a passing grade, he could kiss his place on the hockey team good-bye.

His heart started thudding. Desperately, he scanned the paper again. This time, he saw something he hadn't seen before. He looked more closely to be sure he wasn't mistaken. He saw he was right.

The places he remembered correcting were wrong again. But more than that, *new errors had appeared!*

This isn't the paper I left with the substitute, he realized. It's been changed.

Yet the handwriting looked like his. How could he explain that away?

It's not the first time you've seen something in your handwriting that you knew you didn't write, a little voice inside his head said. The saboteur has struck again. Whoever wrote the note to Kevin also tampered with this paper.

But how was he supposed to convince Ms. Collins of that? And what was she supposed to do even if she did believe him? He still owed her a composition.

Suddenly, an idea struck him. It was his only chance. It would make him a little late — maybe a lot late — for practice, but there was no other possible way.

After class he tried to explain the situation to his teacher.

"Uh, Ms. Collins," he began. He told her how hard he had been working with Beth Ledbetter, how he had written the composition and given it to Beth to look over before handing it in, and how he had his suspicions that someone had messed with it while Ms. Collins had been away. "It's just not what I wrote," he finished.

"I must say I was surprised when I saw it," Ms. Collins admitted. "And disappointed. Beth Ledbetter is far too good a tutor for you to do *worse* after working with her. But Jeff," she added, "that handwriting is so much like yours. I don't know what to make of it."

Jeff cleared his throat. "Well, what if we just pretend it doesn't exist? If you can spare a little time, what if I come back here after school today and write a new composition in front of you? That way you'll be able to see for yourself how I've improved."

Ms. Collins lifted an eyebrow. "But Jeffrey, won't staying after school interfere with hockey?"

Jeff returned her grin. "As someone once told me, sometimes you have to train your mind as well as your body. So what do you say?"

"It's a deal. Be back here at two-thirty sharp."

Jeff nodded, gathered up his books, and rushed to his next class.

Well, that's one problem taken care of, he thought. That leaves two to go: getting Kevin to believe me, and finding out who's trying to do me in!

When the bell rang signaling the end of his last class, Jeff hurried back to Ms. Collins's room. As he turned a corner, he bumped right into Kevin.

Kevin frowned and started to move around him.

"Kevin, wait! I know you're still mad at me, but I really need your help." When he saw Kevin hesitate, he blundered on. "Can you tell Coach I'm going to be a little late to practice? I — I have to meet with my English teacher."

Kevin grimaced. "Your English teacher? Are you in trouble in that class again?"

"I don't know for sure. That's what I have to go find out. Please help me?"

Kevin sighed loudly. "Yeah, sure, I'll tell him. While I'm at it, should I let Sam Metcalf know his chances of suiting up next game are looking pretty good?"

"Just deliver the message to the coach, okay? And Kevin," he added, "I'm going to find out who wrote that note."

But Kevin was already walking away.

Shaking his head, Jeff hurried the rest of the way to Ms. Collins's room. While she sat at her desk correcting papers, he took a seat, pulled a fresh sheet of notebook paper out of his three-ring binder, and began to write. The clock on the wall behind his teacher's desk ticked away the minutes, one by one. But Jeff barely heard it.

He quickly filled the page, then put his pencil down.

Now I have to remember what Beth taught me. I have to go back over it and make sure that I've done everything right. *All the clues are there.*

Beth had been talking about writing when she had said that, but Jeff realized the same statement could be applied to finding his saboteur. With a smile, he set to work on ferreting out the mistakes he'd made on the paper.

He pored over his work carefully. He made some erasures, fixed spelling, and then he rewrote parts of it — until finally he was finished. Half an hour had passed.

He stood up and handed his paper to Ms. Collins. "Here it is. Every single word of it is mine."

Ms. Collins nodded. "Care to stick around while I correct it?"

Jeff sat down again. For the next few moments, he sat tensely as Ms. Collins's green marker moved above his paper. He couldn't tell how many times she used it to make a mark, but she seemed to be examining every letter with extreme care.

That's what I should be doing, Jeff thought. Only the paper I should be checking over is that phony composition. If it hadn't been for that, I'd be over at the skating rink by now!

He pulled out the green ink–filled page and looked at it closely for a third time. And that's when he saw them.

They were faint, but they were there. Little red check marks down the side of the margin.

This wasn't the paper he had turned in. This was the first draft of the composition!

Hold on, he thought. That draft is still in the front pocket of my notebook, isn't it?

He whipped through the pocket quickly. He found an old science test, the start of a letter to Eric Stone, and some doodles, but no first draft.

Beads of perspiration formed on his forehead.

Slowly. Don't jump to any conclusions. Take another look.

He forced himself to be very careful as he turned each page again.

There was no doubt about it. The paper Beth had corrected was missing. Somehow or other, it had found its way onto Ms. Collins's desk.

But how?

No, not *how*, Jeff thought suddenly. *Who*. Who would have known that I had a draft of it in my notebook and why would he have swapped the two? And is it the same person who left that note for Kevin?

Suddenly, Jeff recalled the time he had found Sam squatting over his duffel bag. He had taken Sam's explanation of mistaken identity at face value then. But now he wondered. The compositions had been in his duffel that day. What if Sam had seen them, taken the draft for some reason, then tampered with it? They did play the same position, after all, and what had happened to Jeff the year before when he had failed English was common team knowledge.

I'd do just about anything to get on the squad. Isn't that what Sam had said?

His thoughts were interrupted by Ms. Collins.

"Well done, Jeffrey," she said, beaming. "This is excellent work. It shows a great deal of promise. I knew you could do it."

"Is it — is it good enough to give me a passing grade?" Jeff asked nervously.

"Definitely. As a matter of fact, what are you doing lingering here? Don't you have a practice this afternoon?"

"I sure do! Thanks, Ms. Collins! Thanks a lot!"

Jeff raced to the locker room and suited up in record time. He didn't bother snapping the rubber runners onto his skates, he just dashed into the rink, ready to join the others on the ice.

To his surprise, everyone was seated in the stands. Coach Wallace had obviously called for a break.

"Well, nice of you to join us," the coach said, looking at his watch.

"Didn't Kevin tell you I was going to be late?" Jeff held his breath while he waited for the answer.

"He mumbled something about your being delayed by your English teacher," said the coach. "Since you're here, I guess that means you didn't lose your eligibility."

"No, I definitely did not. Despite what certain people may think, I am still on the team!"

A few heads turned in his direction. Jeff returned their looks straight on before shifting his gaze back to the coach.

Coach Wallace cleared his throat. "Well, glad to hear it," he said mildly. "Now then, Blades, let's run a few more drills before we break down and scrimmage."

As the boys clambered off the benches to the ice, Jeff caught up to Kevin.

"Thanks for delivering my message," he said.

Kevin shrugged.

"Listen," Jeff continued. "Do you still have that note? I'd like to take another look at it."

Kevin stared at him. "I've got it at home, as a matter of fact. Though why I haven't burned it yet, I don't know."

Jeff gave him a small smile. "Maybe it's because you were hoping I'd be able to figure out who really wrote it. You knew you shouldn't destroy the evidence!"

"Maybe," Kevin replied gruffly. "Anyway, if you really think it'll do any good, I guess you can come over to my house after dinner and see it."

Jeff gave a silent cheer. Then he turned his attention back to practice.

Coach had set them up for a passing drill. He wanted them to concentrate on giving and receiving strong, accurate passes. As always, he stressed the importance of letting the stick give at the moment of contact. A bad "catch" could send the puck off in any direction.

Jeff turned in a fine performance in both forehand and backhand passing. When the drill switched to shots on goal, he made sure his were lightning quick. The last set of drills involved dodging a defenseman while carrying the puck, then skimming a pass off to a teammate. Jeff had little trouble with that exercise, either.

But throughout the various plays, Jeff's mind strayed to other things. Like what he thought he'd find when he looked at Kevin's note again — and how he hoped it would prove beyond a doubt that he was innocent.

20

Jeff rushed through dinner that night. He excused himself as soon as he could and mumbled that he had to see Kevin about something.

"That's fine," his mother said. "I've been wondering if there was something going on between you two. I haven't seen Kevin around for a while."

"Everything is fine. Or at least, it will be," Jeff answered. Then he jammed his hat on his head, zipped up his coat, and grabbed his book bag.

Inside were his notebook, the mysterious first draft of the composition, and the one he had just written that afternoon for Ms. Collins.

When he rang Kevin's doorbell, the door opened immediately. Kevin stood there with Ranger at his side.

Jeff took a deep breath. Then he did something he had never thought he would do. He held his hand out toward Ranger's nose.

Ranger sniffed it. Jeff slowly moved his hand from in front of Ranger's nose to the top of Ranger's head — and patted him!

Ranger's tail thumped and Kevin's eyes widened. "Well, I'll be," he said. He stepped aside to let Jeff in. "Come on up."

Kevin led the way to his bedroom. The note was lying on his desk. Jeff picked it up eagerly.

At a glance, he saw his instincts had been right. And he knew that there was no way Sam Metcalf was involved. Without a word, he set it back down on the desk and unzipped his book bag. He withdrew his notebook, opened the three rings, and took out a blank sheet of paper. Then he dug out the two compositions. Finally, he laid the note alongside them.

With a gesture of his hand, he asked Kevin to compare the four pieces of paper.

Kevin took a moment, then shrugged. "I don't get it. If I'm supposed to be comparing the handwriting, I still can't see a difference. But what's the blank page for?"

Jeff just said, "The clues are all there. Keep looking and I think you'll see for yourself."

So Kevin looked again. And this time he saw what Jeff meant.

"This, this, and this," he said, pointing to the two compositions and the note, "are all two-hole-punched pieces of paper. But this one," he finished, picking up the blank sheet, "is a three-hole."

"Right," said Jeff. "Now, you know that that blank sheet came from my notebook, because you saw me take it from there. But that other paper is different." Jeff picked up the note. "The ink used in the lines is a funny shade of blue. It's almost purple. The paper feels smoother, too. I've only seen paper like that once before."

"Where?"

"In Beth Ledbetter's notebook. Her dad gave her a special binder filled with it last year."

Kevin stared at Jeff in amazement. "You mean *Beth Ledbetter* wrote this note? I don't believe it!"

"No, not Beth," Jeff said. "But someone who has a binder with paper just like hers. That someone had to know an awful lot in

143

order to write that note. He had to know that Beth was tutoring me, that I had written a make-up composition, and that my topic had been about you and Ranger. And since I'm pretty sure whoever wrote that note also sabotaged my make-up composition," he finished sadly, "that someone also had to know what would happen to me if I got a failing grade."

"You sound like you already know who it is," Kevin said.

"I think I do. But I'll need your help to prove it." Then he told Kevin who he thought the perpetrator was and why he had done it. Kevin whistled.

"If it's true, then he's in for some big trouble," he said.

"I know. But even though he messed things up between you and me, I wish there was some way of keeping him out of it. But he brought it on himself. No one forced him."

"So what now?"

"Now, I think we have to come up with a plan for flushing the criminal out."

The boys talked for the next hour. Then Jeff got up to leave.

"I'll see you tomorrow, Kevin. Pick you up at seven-thirty to go to school. Okay?"

"Tell you what," Kevin replied. "Come by at seven and help me walk Ranger."

Jeff grinned. "You got a deal."

21

Classes flew by the next day. When practice started, Jeff and Kevin put their plan into action. It started with a fight.

"That stupid dog of yours tipped over our garbage cans this morning," Jeff said to Kevin. He punctuated his accusation by poking a finger into Kevin's chest.

"Did not!" Kevin replied angrily. "You probably tipped them yourself just so you could blame Ranger!"

"It would serve him right if he became known as a menace to the neighborhood."

"Oh, so you admit you tipped them?"

"No! But it's probably just a matter of time before he proves what a worthless, mean mutt he is. He'll bite someone or bark his head off all night or chase people on bikes. Your flea-bitten mongrel will get what he deserves soon enough!"

Kevin spun on his heel and stomped to his locker. The other boys looked at each other uneasily.

"What's all that shouting?" Coach Wallace entered the locker room holding his clipboard. "Well?"

"Nothing, Coach," a few of the boys mumbled.

"Then what are you all lollygagging around for? Get suited up and out on the ice! Pronto!"

As Jeff headed for the door, he saw Kevin hold the door open for Hayes and Bucky.

Bucky seemed to be badgering Hayes about something. Hayes just shook his head but didn't say anything.

Coach Wallace had the team set up for a scrimmage immediately after warm-up. The lineup was as usual: Chad, Bucky, and Jeff in the front, Shep and Kevin backing them up, and Michael in the cage.

The coach played referee and dropped the puck for the face-off. Bucky controlled it right away and sent it skimming to Chad. Chad skated with it for a few feet, then lateraled it back to Bucky. Bucky dodged a defenseman, glanced up, and found Jeff in the clear.

Jeff stopped the puck easily, but instead of taking off down the ice with it, he slowed his pace. His heart pounded. Okay, Kevin, he said to himself, here we go.

As if he had heard Jeff's thoughts, Kevin

started skating furiously. Jeff turned a blind shoulder to him and braced himself.

Wham!

Kevin hit Jeff full force and sent him reeling. Jeff collided with the boards and fell hard. He didn't get up.

Coach Wallace blew his whistle. All action stopped as he sped over to the prone figure.

Jeff sat up, looking dazed. He stood slowly but winced as he put weight on his left foot.

"I — I think it's sprained, Coach," he said weakly.

"Kevin, help Jeff into the locker room," Coach Wallace said.

"No," Kevin said in a low voice.

Shocked, Coach Wallace stared at him. "What do you mean, *no!*"

"Not until he confesses."

The coach looked baffled. "Confesses what? What's this all about?"

"Confesses that he put a bunch of mean notes threatening my dog in my locker! I've been getting one every day this week!"

"*What?*"

This time, it wasn't the coach who had spoken. It was Bucky Ledbetter.

Coach Wallace turned to him. "Do you know what's happening here, Bucky?" he asked.

Bucky swallowed hard. "I — I'm not sure. I mean, I know a little of it, but that's all."

Coach Wallace continued to look at him. Bucky dug his skate into the ice. "I should have said something sooner, but I didn't know how. And I thought it was only that one time. I didn't know it had been going on longer."

He looked up and shot a glance at his brother.

The coach caught the look. So did everyone else. Hayes stood there, his head hung low.

"It was me," he mumbled. Then he lifted his head. "But I only put one note in Kevin's locker. One! I don't know where the other ones came from."

Jeff moved forward. "There were no other ones. Kevin and I just pretended there were, hoping you'd come forward to deny it."

"And it worked," Kevin added.

Jeff nodded. "You got pretty good at my handwriting, Hayes. But how?"

"I — I found part of a composition you'd written in my sister's trash can. I traced some of it. Changed words from what you had written until it was the note Kevin got."

Bucky cut in. "I caught him doing it," he confessed. "I should have stopped him, but he told me it was just a joke. By the time I realized it wasn't, it was too late."

Jeff shook his head. "You might have gotten away with it, Hayes. But you forged my writing again, didn't you? By replacing my good composition with one you had tampered with?"

"Yeah." Hayes sounded defeated. "I grabbed your draft out of your notebook while you were giving the real one to the substitute. Then I just changed a few things and switched them later that week."

"Why'd you do it, Hayes? What did I ever do to you?"

Then it all came out. "You stood in my way. I didn't make the team last year because of you. Then you got thrown off and I was still sitting in the stands! Now this year, when you shouldn't have even been allowed to try out, you're playing first string."

"But you made the team this year and you're subbing in all the time!" Jeff said in amazement.

"Yeah, but how long can that continue? We all know there's a better player just waiting for me to slip up." Hayes's eyes slid over to Sam Metcalf.

Sam looked startled. "Gee, Hayes, I guess I can't deny that I'd rather be a full-time player than an alternate. But I want to earn my uniform, not get it because someone was thrown off!"

Coach Wallace put a heavy hand on Hayes's shoulder. "Hayes, I think you better go to the locker room. I'll be there in a moment. The rest of you, set up a shooting drill."

Hayes slumped, then skated slowly away. The other boys silently shuffled into place for the drill. Once it was going, Coach Wallace started toward the locker room.

Jeff broke out of his line and caught up to him. "Coach, what are you going to do with Hayes?" he asked.

153

The coach shook his head. "What do you think, Jeff? I can't let him off the hook."

Jeff looked the coach in the eye. "Please don't kick him off the team," he said quietly. "Hayes made mistakes — big ones — but I can understand what made him do it. I — I know what it's like to worry about keeping your place on the team. And I'd hate for him to go through what I went through last year."

Coach Wallace studied Jeff for a moment. Then he said, "Well, since you were the person most likely to be hurt by what Hayes did, what would you suggest I do?"

"I know Hayes has to be punished. But couldn't you switch him to alternate instead of kicking him off the team altogether? He's really shaping into a good player, and if he gets a season of practices under his belt, I bet he could be a real asset to the team next year. Plus, maybe if the other guys see that you and I are willing to give him another chance, they'll forgive him, too. I know I'll never forget that you gave me another chance."

Jeff held his breath while the coach thought it over. Then he nodded. "Okay, Jeff. If Hayes is willing to move to alternate, then I'll let him stay on."

"Great!" Jeff cried. "Thanks, Coach!"

"Don't thank me. It's your plan. And I'll be sure Hayes knows it. Now get back out there. We've got a game this Saturday and I want all my players to be prepared!"

22

Saturday morning, the snow was flying thick and fast. Mr. and Mrs. Connors drove Jeff to the rink. Even Candy decided to watch the game.

The first thing Jeff noticed when he came into the locker room was that Sam Metcalf was in uniform. And that Sam looked unhappy.

"I just don't feel right, wearing this," he said to Jeff. "I didn't really earn it."

A lull in the chatter made Jeff and Sam turn. Hayes had come in and was walking straight toward them.

"You deserve to wear that more than I do," he said. "You've been practicing just as hard as any of us."

Hayes turned to Jeff. "Coach told me what you said. Thanks for giving me another chance."

"Hey, I know what it's like to feel insecure about something. For me, it's writing. And dogs, too, I guess, though I'm getting over that with help from Kevin and Ranger. For you, it was your ability to play good hockey. But both of us are improving. And don't forget, next year Bucky and the other ninth graders move on to high school, which means there will be a few more open spots on the team. Who better than you to fill one of them?"

Hayes cracked a small smile. "Yeah, good point. Well, good luck in the game. Show those Groveland Jets who's boss!"

Ten minutes later, Jeff was on the ice waiting for the referee to drop the puck for the face-off.

The whistle blew and the puck hit the ice. Bucky gained control immediately and shot the disk to Jeff. Jeff captured it and took off into the attack zone.

From behind him, Kevin called out, "I'm with you if you need me!"

Jeff spotted Chad skating neck and neck with his Jets defenseman. Then he broke free and skated quickly toward the goal. With a smooth move, Jeff sent the puck sailing to his stick.

But it was picked off before it reached Chad. The Jets defender dodged around Chad and made a move toward the Blades goal.

He hadn't reckoned on Shep, however. The powerful defenseman slipped in, stole the puck off a bad tap, and passed it cross-ice to Kevin.

Kevin protected the puck by skating close to the boards. Jeff took up position directly in front of him. With a backhand sweep, Kevin sent the puck skimming up to Jeff's waiting stick.

Jeff spotted Bucky skating alongside him. "Three!" Bucky yelled, signaling that they were in prime position to put play number three into motion. With a nod of acknowledgment, Jeff sent the puck to Bucky, then set off.

All Jeff had to do was work his way to about six feet in front of the net and a little off to the right side. Kevin would come skating by him as though he were going to take a pass from Bucky. But he'd let the puck go by him. Then Jeff would grab it, spin around, and slap one into the net. The surprise element was crucial if the play was to succeed.

Everything happened exactly as it should have. Jeff got into position. Bucky held on to the puck. When Kevin made his move, he gave no indication that he was even aware of Jeff's presence. But in contrast to the last game, Jeff knew this was just a ruse. Kevin was playing his part perfectly.

And it worked! Kevin shot past Jeff just as Bucky let the puck fly. Jeff stopped it and a second later sent it sailing into the goal!

Sticks waving madly in the air and cheers erupting from their throats, the Blades crowded around Jeff to congratulate him. Then they quickly got into position for the next face-off.

Jeff turned his head slightly as he waited for the whistle. Out of the corner of his eye, he saw Kevin give him a thumbs-up sign.

Jeff knew that even if the Blades didn't win the game, he was going to go home happy.

When the ref took position for the drop, Jeff couldn't control himself.

"Let's go, you guys!" he yelled. "Let's show 'em who's boss!"

"Heads-up playing!" Kevin joined in.

"Dig in!" echoed Shep.

The whistle blew. The puck dropped. Bucky missed it this time, but Shep acted quickly and intercepted a pass the Jets center tried to make to his wing. Shep skated forward a few feet and passed to Chad.

Chad took long, smooth strokes, carefully controlling his speed and the puck. It seemed as though he were taking his time, that he didn't really care if he brought the puck into scoring position or not.

But his lazy attitude was deceptive. When a Jets defenseman attacked, Chad made a sharp lateral move. The Jets player had so much forward momentum that he rocketed right into the boards behind Chad.

Chad skated calmly forward a few more feet, heading straight toward Bucky.

Jeff knew what was coming. And sure enough, no more than six feet in front of the goal, Chad and Bucky passed each other almost shoulder to shoulder. The puck slipped from Chad's stick to Bucky's. Bucky took up the left-wing position while Chad, pretending to have the puck still, stopped abruptly as if he were about to shoot.

The Jets were fooled for no more than a second. It was long enough for Bucky to sneak into position for a shot on goal. But his attempt failed when the puck ricocheted off the goalie's pads and onto the waiting Jets stick.

Back and forth the play went. By the end of the first period, the shots-on-goal statistics showed that both teams had had many chances to score. But the board still read Blades 1, Jets 0.

At the start of the second period, Coach Wallace subbed in a few players. Jeff and

Bucky came out. Sam and the second-string center went in.

Bucky moved close to Hayes on the bench.

"Listen, little brother," he said. "I hope you can follow Jeff's lead and forgive me."

Hayes stared at his brother.

"For razzing you so hard the beginning of the season," Bucky continued. "I think maybe it had something to do with what you did, huh?"

Hayes shrugged. "Maybe a little," he said. "But no one can take the blame for what I did but me. And at least I'm still part of the team. Sam and Jeff just better look out next year, that's all!"

Jeff grinned at him. "I'll give you a run for your money, just you wait," he promised. "Now let's stop all this true-confessions stuff. We've got a game out there to win!"

The #1
Sports Series
for Kids

Read them all!

*Previously published as Crackerjack Halfback

All available in paperback from Little, Brown and Company

**Previously published as Pressure Play

Matt Christopher®

Sports Bio Bookshelf

Muhammad Ali	Tara Lipinski
Lance Armstrong	Mark McGwire
Kobe Bryant	Yao Ming
Jennifer Capriati	Shaquille O'Neal
Jeff Gordon	Jackie Robinson
Ken Griffey Jr.	Alex Rodriguez
Mia Hamm	Babe Ruth
Tony Hawk	Curt Schilling
Ichiro	Sammy Sosa
Derek Jeter	Venus and Serena Williams
Randy Johnson	
Michael Jordan	Tiger Woods
Mario Lemieux	